BY THE LIGHT OF THE HALLOWEEN MOON

CAROLINE STUTSON • KEVIN HAWKES

Puffin Books

PUFFIN BOOKS
Published by the Penguin Group
Penguin Books USA Inc., 375 Hudson Street, New York, New York 10014, U.S.A.
Penguin Books Ltd, 27 Wrights Lane, London W8 5TZ, England
Penguin Books Australia Ltd, Ringwood, Victoria, Australia
Penguin Books Canada Ltd, 10 Alcorn Avenue, Toronto, Ontario, Canada M4V 3B2
Penguin Books (N.Z.) Ltd, 182-190 Wairau Road, Auckland 10, New Zealand

Penguin Books Ltd, Registered Offices: Harmondsworth, Middlesex, England

First published in the United States of America by Lothrop, Lee, &
Shepard Books, a division of William Morrow & Company, Inc., 1993
Reprinted by arrangement with William Morrow & Company, Inc.
Published in Puffin Books, 1994

10 9

LIBRARY OF CONGRESS CATALOGING-IN-PUBLICATION DATA
Stutson, Caroline.
By the light of the Halloween moon / Caroline Stutson ; [illustrated by] Kevin Hawkes. p. cm.
Summary: In this cumulative story, a host of Halloween spooks,
including a cat, a witch, and a ghoul, are drawn to the tapping of a little girl's toe.
ISBN 0-14-055305-3
1. Halloween—Fiction. 2. Stories in rhyme. 3. II lb11 04-18-94.] I. Hawkes, Kevin, ill. II. Title.
PZ8.3.S925By 1994 [E]—dc20 94-15987 CIP AC

Printed in the United States of America

For A.C., Chris, Al, and Randy–C.S.
For Susan Pearson–K.H.

A toe!
A lean and gleaming toe
That taps a tune in the dead of night
By the light, by the light,
By the silvery light of the Halloween moon!

A cat!
A thin black wisp of a spying cat
Who eyes the toe
That taps a tune in the dead of night
By the light, by the light,
By the silvery light of the Halloween moon!

A witch!
A watchful witch with streaming hair
Who snatches the cat
When he springs through the air to catch the toe
That taps a tune in the dead of night
By the light, by the light,
By the silvery light of the Halloween moon!

A bat!
A bungling bouncy breezy bat

Who bumps the witch as she snatches the cat
When he springs through the air to catch the toe
That taps a tune in the dead of night
By the light, by the light,
By the silvery light of the Halloween moon!

A ghoul!
A ghastly drooling graveyard ghoul

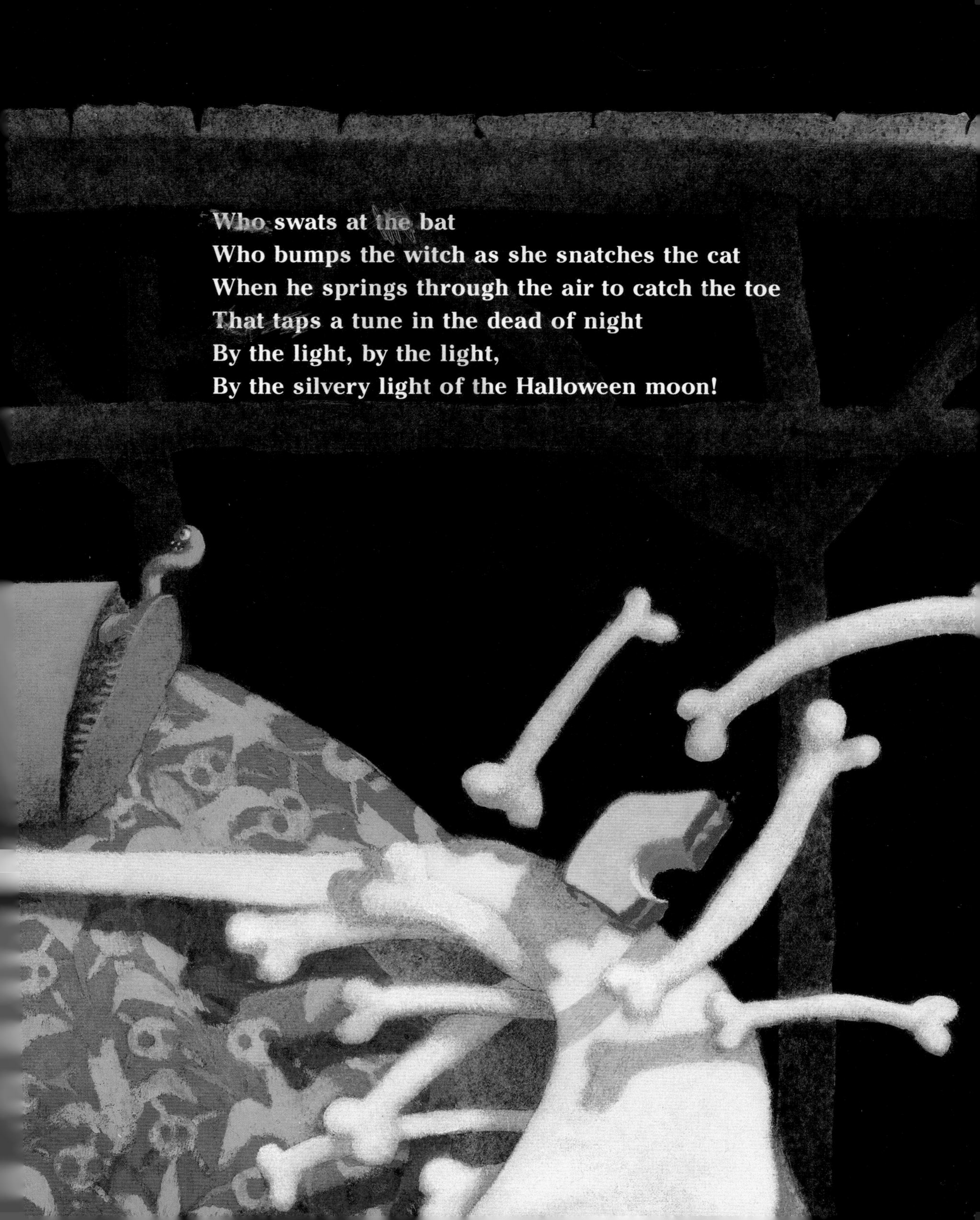

Who swats at the bat
Who bumps the witch as she snatches the cat
When he springs through the air to catch the toe
That taps a tune in the dead of night
By the light, by the light,
By the silvery light of the Halloween moon!

A ghost!
A williwaw ghost

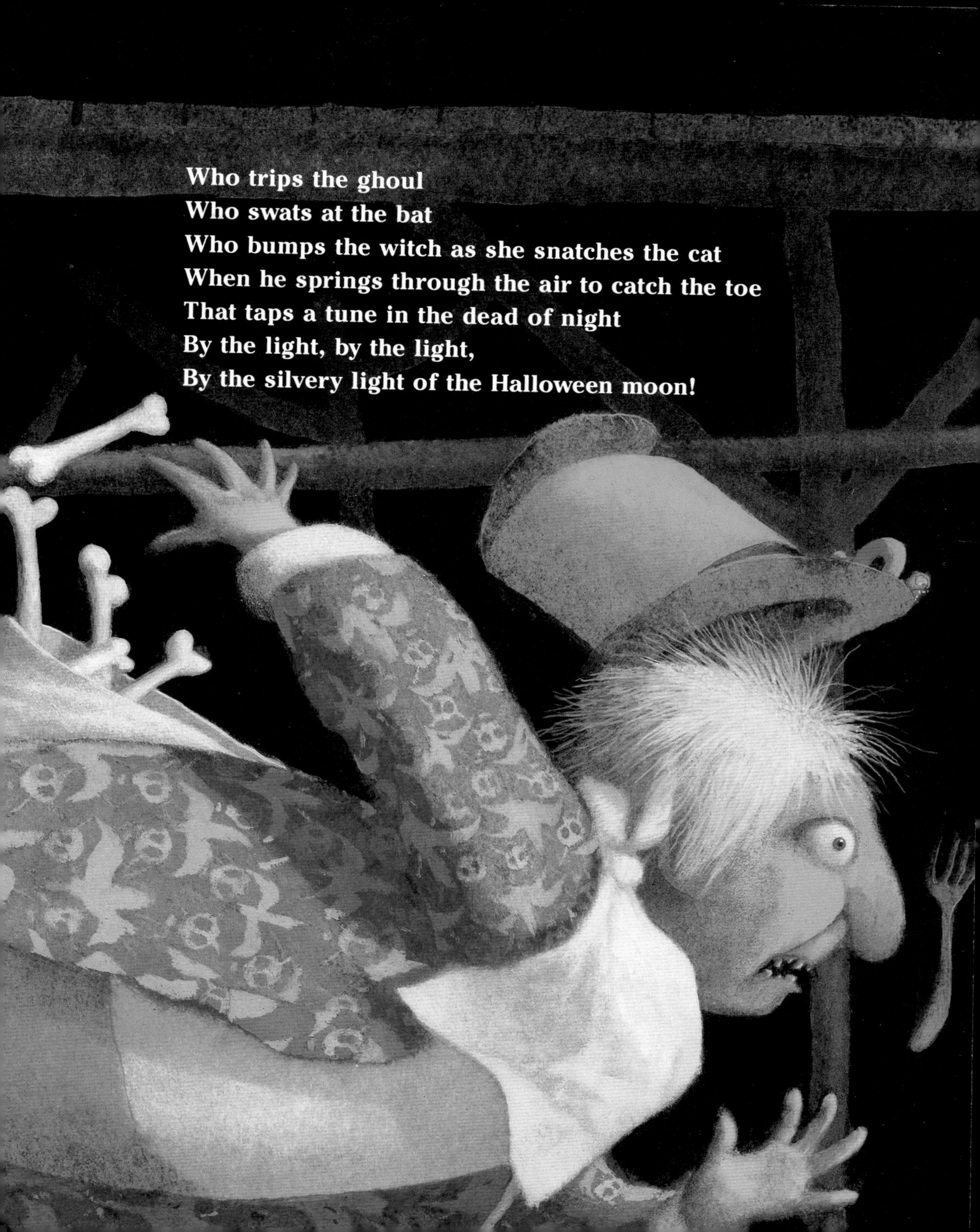

Who trips the ghoul
Who swats at the bat
Who bumps the witch as she snatches the cat
When he springs through the air to catch the toe
That taps a tune in the dead of night
By the light, by the light,
By the silvery light of the Halloween moon!

A sprite!
A grumpy grungy hobgoblin sprite

Who bites the ghost
Who trips the ghoul
Who swats at the bat
Who bumps the witch as she snatches the cat
When he springs through the air to catch the toe
That taps a tune in the dead of night
By the light, by the light,
By the silvery light of the Halloween moon!

A girl!
A small bright slip of a smiling girl

Who smacks the sprite
Who bites the ghost
Who trips the ghoul
Who swats at the bat
Who bumps the witch as she snatches the cat
When he springs through the air to catch the toe
That taps a tune in the dead of night

By the light, by the light,
By the silvery light of the Halloween moon!